Motorcycles: Made for Speed!™

CHOPPERS

Connor Dayton

PowerKiDS
press™

New York

Published in 2007 by The Rosen Publishing Group, Inc.
29 East 21st Street, New York, NY 10010

First Edition

Editor: Jennifer Way
Book Design: Erica Clendening
Layout Design: Kate Laczynski
Photo Researcher: Sam Cha

Photo Credits: Cover, pp. 9, 11, 21, 23 © Getty Images; pp. 1, 5, 7, 13, 15, 17, 19 © www.shutterstock.com.

Library of Congress Cataloging-in-Publication Data

Dayton, Connor.
  Choppers / Connor Dayton. — 1st ed.
      p. cm. — (Motorcycles—made for speed)
  Includes index.
  ISBN-13: 978-1-4042-3654-7 (library binding)
  ISBN-10: 1-4042-3654-6 (library binding)
  1. Motorcycles—Customizing—Juvenile literature. 2. Home built motorcycles—Juvenile literature. I. Title.
TL440.15.D387 2007
629.227'5—dc22
                                              2006023978

Manufactured in the United States of America

Contents

A chopper is a type of street motorcycle that has been **customized**. This makes it look and ride differently from other bikes.

5

Most choppers have wider handlebars than other motorcycles. They also have lower seats.

Choppers often have front wheels that are set far out in front. This helps the chopper's rider sit close to the ground.

A chopper's back wheel is fatter than the front wheel. Chopper wheels often have lots of shiny **chrome** spokes.

11

Another place on a chopper where you can see lots of chrome is on the tailpipes.

13

Choppers often have custom paint jobs. Sometimes the paint job will be a cool picture. It may also be a fun color.

15

Choppers have **gauges** that help riders make sure they are riding at a safe speed.

Choppers are customized in different ways. This chopper has a space-age look.

19

Like other bikers, chopper riders wear helmets to stay safe on the road.

Sometimes chopper owners meet up to ride together. It is fun for them to ride as a group and to show off their customized bikes.

23

Glossary

chrome (KROHM) A shiny metal that is used on motorcycles.

customized (KUS-tum-eyzd) Made in a certain way for a person.

gauges (GAYJ-ez) Things that tell facts about something.

Index

Web Sites

Due to the changing nature of Internet links, PowerKids Press has developed an online list of Web sites related to this book. This site is updated regularly. Please use this link to access the list:

www.powerkidslinks.com/motor/choppers/